LOOK, I'M DOUBLE "U"!

For Claire and Lizzie
   —J. T.

For Simone and Alayna
   —D. C.

With thanks to Laurie Keller
   and Kathleen Wright
   and Dawn Anderson
   and Beth McLampy
   and Carroll Hart
   and Melissa Chinchillo
   and Christy Ottaviano
   and sometimes Y

Henry Holt and Company, LLC
Publishers since 1866
175 Fifth Avenue
New York, New York 10010
www.HenryHoltKids.com

Henry Holt® is a registered trademark
of Henry Holt and Company, LLC.
Text copyright © 2009 by James Tobin
Illustrations copyright © 2009 by Dave Coverly
All rights reserved.
Distributed in Canada by H. B. Fenn and Company Ltd.

Library of Congress Cataloging-in-Publication Data
Tobin, James.
Sue MacDonald had a book / Jim Tobin ;
illustrated by Dave Coverly.—1st ed.
p.   cm.
Summary: When A, E, I, O, and U jump off the page,
reader Sue MacDonald pursues the renegade vowels.
ISBN-13: 978-0-8050-8766-6
ISBN-10: 0-8050-8766-4
[1. Stories in rhyme. 2. English language—Vowels—Fiction.]
I. Coverly, Dave, ill. II. Title.
PZ8.3.T5555Su 2009
[E]—dc22
2008018338

First Edition—2009
Designed by Elynn Cohen
The artist used ink and watercolors on Arches 90-lb. hot-press
watercolor paper to create the illustrations for this book.
Printed in China on acid-free paper. ∞

10 9 8 7 6 5 4 3 2 1

SUE MACDONALD
Had a Book

Jim Tobin • illustrated by Dave Coverly

Christy Ottaviano Books
Henry Holt and Company
New York

Sue MacDonald had a book.

The words made sense
last time she looked.
AEIOU

But **A** grabbed **E**
and said, "We're free!"

I and **O** said, "Let's go!"

U said, "Gee, guys, I don't know."

Sue MacDonald had a book.
Now what will she do?

Sue MacDonald chased her **A**.

A E I O U

He laughed
and then he ran away.

He hopped a train
and rode to Maine.

Far away, took all day,
ticket taker made him pay.

Sue MacDonald caught her **A**.
After **A**, then who?

Sue MacDonald searched for E.

AEIOU

She saw him sleeping in a tree.

AEIOU

She wove a net and got all set.

Big trapeze, flew with ease . . .

...tossed him to the chimpanzees.

Sue MacDonald found her E.
After E, then who?

Sue MacDonald spied her **I**.

AEIOU

She watched him climb up to the sky.

AEIOU

He tried to hide;
she hitched a ride.

Scary climb, nick of time,
saved him from a life of crime.

Sue MacDonald rescued **I**.
After **I**, then who?

Sue MacDonald followed O.

A E I O U

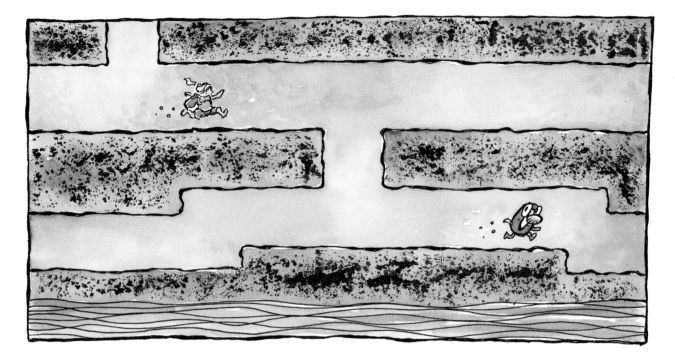

They dropped down where the microbes grow.

AEIOU

MICROBES NOT ACTUAL SIZE

O slipped in slop
and stopped to mop.

On a roll, down a hole,
caught him with a fishing pole.

Sue MacDonald hooked her O.
After O, then who?

Sue MacDonald hunted U

AEIOU

from Kansas U. . .

to Katmandu.

AEIOU

She felt a tug and got a hug.

Sue MacDonald
had her book and
all her vowels, too.

Sue MacDonald went to bed.

AEIOU

She sounded out the words she read.

AEIOU

With A and E
and $I, O, U,$
see if you can read them, too.

Sue MacDonald had a book . . .

. . . and sometimes Y.

LOOK, I'M "C"!